Space Dogs
on
Planet K-9

Space Dogs on Planet K-9

by Joan Holub
illustrated by Mike Reed

To my wonderful husband, George—
thanks for listening to my ideas.
— J.H.

To Joe and Alex
—M.R.

Contents

Chapter 1

Outer-Space Nightmare

Clark stepped onto the stage, grinning proudly. His baseball team had won the state championship, and the coach was handing the trophy to him.

He reached out for it.

Suddenly he felt a tingle—sort of like static electricity—spread quickly through his body.

He glanced down in horror. He was disappearing!

". . .Where am I?" Clark groaned, opening one eye halfway.

Dumb question. He was sitting at a desk.

Correction. On *top* of a desk—a teacher's desk at the front of a classroom.

But how had he gotten there?

His eyes popped wide open, and he looked around. About twenty giant dogs sat gaping at him from desks lined up in rows. There were dogs of almost every breed—all of them about three times bigger than normal dogs.

"Wow," said a giant beagle standing next to him. "I didn't know you could talk!"

"Hey, Roid, what else can it say?" one of the other dogs asked the beagle.

Roid the beagle nudged Clark. "Say something else," he whispered.

Strangely enough, the dogs glowed neon green every time they spoke—and they stood on two feet instead of four.

Suddenly Clark slumped in relief. Now he got it. This must be another one of his dreams about aliens. He had them all the time.

"Is this a dream?" Clark asked.

Roid scratched his ear. The other dog aliens gasped or clapped like it was some big deal that Clark could talk.

Bowoooo! A horrible howling bark sounded

over the intercom. It echoed around the room, bouncing off the walls.

Clark clutched his head in pain. "What was that?" he moaned.

"The school's-out woof," Roid replied, shrugging as though it were nothing unusual.

A huge poodle came in, toes clicking on the shiny floor. "Okay, Sharing Time is over. For tonight's homework assignment, list your twenty favorite places to bury bones and why. See you all tomorrow." The poodle clicked back out.

"Come on," Roid said, picking Clark up. "We have to get home before Aster does." He put Clark in a box with holes in the sides and handles and closed the lid.

"I told Mom that Aster didn't waste her money on you," Roid went on, peeking in through the holes at Clark. "You've turned out even better than I expected."

Roid picked up the box and started walking. Knocked off balance, Clark slammed into its side.

You weren't supposed to feel pain in dreams, were you? Clark asked himself. Maybe—just maybe—this *wasn't* a dream.

None of his dreams had ever seemed this real before, that was for sure!

Clark bounced around inside the box, worrying until he finally couldn't stand it anymore. He banged on the box lid.

Roid came to a sudden halt. He lifted the lid and stared in at Clark. "What?"

"Let me out of here," Clark complained.

"Do you want me to put on your leash instead?" asked Roid.

"No!" Clark replied impatiently.

"It's the box or the leash," said Roid. "That's the law."

"Okay then—the leash," Clark decided. Anything had to be better than the box.

Roid set the box down and got out a woven leash and a collar like the ones Clark had for his dog, Critter. He fastened the collar around Clark's neck. Clark made a gagging sound.

"Too tight?" asked Roid.

Clark nodded, and Roid loosened it.

"Come on now," Roid said, tugging on the leash. "We've got to get a wiggle on."

"Where am I?" Clark asked once again, trotting alongside Roid.

Roid gave him a weird look. "Where do you think?"

"In New Jersey?"

"Is that someplace on planet Ick?" asked Roid.

"Ick? I'm from planet Earth," said Clark.

"We call your planet 'Ick,'" Roid explained.

"Ick, Earth, whatever—is that where I am now?" Clark wondered.

"No. You're on planet K-9, two galaxies away from there. I took you to school for Sharing Day, and now we're headed back home."

Roid came to an abrupt stop. He leaned down, wagging a finger at Clark's nose. "But remember," he cautioned, "if Aster asks, you were *never* at school with me."

Roid took off again. With the leash around his neck, Clark had no choice but to follow.

"Who's Aster?" he asked.

"My flea-bitten sister, that's who," said Roid. "You're hers, and she'll hit the stars if she finds out I borrowed you."

"What do you mean I'm 'hers'?" Clark demanded.

"Aster bought you from the Interplanetary Shopping Network two days ago. Don't you remember your trip from Ick?"

"Trip? No, I don't remember any trip," Clark said.

"Well, come to think of it," Roid recalled, "you have been in sort of a trance since Aster got you. They probably freeze-dried you for transport. It must have taken until today for you to snap out of it."

"Wait a minute—are you saying that I'm your sister's slave or something?" Clark gasped.

"Slave? No! What do you think we are around here? K-9-ians don't have slaves," Roid protested. "Do you know what a pet is?"

"Yeah . . ." Clark answered slowly. A horrible thought began forming in his mind.

"Well, you," said Roid, "are Aster's pet."

Chapter 2

Here, Clark-y, Clark-y

Clark was stunned into silence.

"Don't look so worried," said Roid. "You'll be mine soon if I have my way."

"I don't want to be yours," Clark argued.

"Why not? You'll be better off with me. Aster is horrible with pets."

"What do you mean—horrible?"

Roid shrugged. "You know, forgets to feed them. Doesn't play with them. That kind of stuff."

Roid hopped on a moving sidewalk, so Clark was forced to do likewise. He had ridden them before at the airport. This one took them through a tunnel, then all the way to Roid's house in no time.

The biggest beagle Clark had ever seen greeted them at the door. It turned out to be Roid's mom.

"What are you doing with Aster's Ickie?" she wanted to know.

"Uh, I took it for a walk," Roid fibbed. "You know how Aster forgets to take care of her pets."

"Did you figure out if it's house-trained?" she asked.

Roid cocked his head and looked at Clark.

Clark rolled his eyes. He didn't really want to get into a discussion of his bathroom habits. He gave Roid a tiny nod.

"Yes, it is," Roid told her.

"Are its paws clean?" Roid's mother asked.

Roid lifted Clark's feet and examined the bottoms of his shoes. "Yes," he said.

She sighed. "Okay, bring it in. I still wish Aster hadn't insisted on getting an Ickie. A Plutonian Wiggler would've been a better choice. Oh, well, that's water under the dogtrot now. Don't forget—dinner is in an hour." Her voice faded as she padded into the next room.

"Okay," Roid called after her, tugging Clark toward the stairs. Clark pulled the collar and leash off on the way up.

"Where and how exactly did Aster buy me?" he asked, once they got to Roid's room.

The room was a mess. The floor was made of tiny glittering rocks, like the ones found on the bottoms of fish tanks. There were holes dug everywhere, and chew toys all over the place.

"I told you—from the Interplanetary Shopping Network. Here, I'll show you," said Roid.

He flicked a button on a remote-control device. It switched on a huge TV screen that was built into the wall. It also turned on an anti-gravity machine. Roid and Clark were soon both floating in front of the screen in comfort.

"This is cool," Clark said.

"Saves wear and tear on the body," Roid agreed.

He punched some more buttons. The TV whirred and hummed.

Zap! A smiling salesdog appeared on the screen. His image was 3-D, so he almost seemed to leap out into the room as he began yelling:

"... Now YOU can own the home version of FETCH, the hilarious game that will 'bow-WOW' your friends. ..."

Roid flicked the button again, and the image changed to another salesdog.

"... Do you find yourself feeling dog-tired? Try WOOF-IT-UP, the amazing new product that will have you woofing it up in no time. ..."

Roid pushed another button, and the image changed yet again.

"There!" Roid shouted, pointing toward the screen. Clark stared at it in horror.

". . . INSTANT ICKIES! Be the first on your block to own one. They are loads of fun. A dog's best friend . . ." shouted a smiling salesdog with perfect teeth.

He held up a picture. Of Clark! They were selling Earth kids as pets and using his picture to advertise them!

". . . Your Ickie will arrive freeze-dried. All you do is add water. We sold out of our first offering of ten Ickies. But we'll have a new shipment in a few weeks. So don't wait. Order yours today! . . ."

Ten! thought Clark. Wait a minute—there were ten players on his baseball team. The whole team must have been kidnapped at once! But where were all the others?

"Hey!" a voice shrieked. "My Ickie's gone!"

"Uh-oh," said Roid, hunching his shoulders. "It's Aster." He clicked off the screen, and they both sank gently to the floor.

Roid turned to Clark with a calculating look on his face. "Don't speak in front of her, okay? She'll never let me have you if she finds out you can talk."

Suddenly a scowling beagle skidded to a halt just inside Roid's door. "I knew it!" Aster cried. "*You* stole my Ickie!"

"I was only playing with it," Roid protested.

Aster snatched Clark by the back of his shirt and stuck him under her arm. "If you want one, buy your own," she told Roid. "Because this one is mine!" And with that, she stomped out.

Clark dangled at Aster's side until they reached her room. There she stuck him in a large wire cage and then promptly forgot about him.

She turned on some music and began dancing. "How much is that Plutonian Wiggler in the window?" she howled along with the music. Clark covered his ears and was glad she left a few minutes later to eat dinner. Once she got back, she gazed in her mirror, combing her hair and tying little bows in it for what seemed like hours.

Clark had news for her. No matter how much she did to herself, she would *never* win any beauty contests. But he wasn't about to tell her.

After a while it grew dark. Aster curled up in a big round basket bed and went to sleep.

Clark was bored sitting in the dark cage. No comic books. No video games. No nothing! And how was he supposed to sleep without a blanket and pillow?

Worst of all—he was thirsty. And starving!

But his brain must have been on overload, because in spite of everything, Clark eventually fell asleep.

Chapter 3

Aster Disaster

The next thing Clark knew, a voice was nudging him awake.

"Rise and shine, Ickie," Roid singsonged.

"Water," croaked Clark. "I'm dying of thirst."

Roid let Clark out of his cage and gave him some water in a bowl. "I just can't get over you being able to talk, Ickie," he said happily.

"Clark. My name is Clark," said Clark, once he'd drunk most of the water.

"Quark?" Roid replied. "Okay, Quark it is."

Clark started to correct him, but just then

Aster zoomed in. "I told you to stay away from my Ickie!" she shouted.

"But it looked thirsty," said Roid.

"And hungry," Clark whispered, so only Roid could hear.

"And hungry," repeated Roid, more loudly.

"Oh," Aster said. "I guess I forgot to feed it last night."

She started digging through her closet. "Now where'd I put that Ickie food the Bonezillion brothers sold me? . . . Here it is. Would you feed it for me?" she whined, thrusting a box into Roid's hands. "Honestly, pets are such a pain sometimes."

"Why don't you sell it if you're tired of it?" Roid asked. He opened the cage and put Clark, the water bowl, and the food inside.

Clark gobbled down a handful of the food. Dry cereal. Yuck.

"I might," said Aster.

"I'll buy it from you," offered Roid.

But he made the mistake of sounding too eager. Aster smelled profit. She squinted her beady beagle eyes at him. "If it's such a crummy pet, why do you want it?"

"I just feel bad because I talked you into

buying it. And then it turned out to be a dud," said Roid, more casually.

"Maybe I'll think about it. But it looks more awake than before, even if it isn't as much fun as the Bonezillion brothers salesdogs made it sound on TV. So I'm keeping it for now. And that means paws off, glow dog! Now get out of my room."

Aster opened the door and waited until Roid had gone past. Then she whirled out after him, slamming the door shut behind them.

Clark kept on munching the food Roid had given him. No milk. No spoon. Just dry cereal from a box. Gross. But he was so hungry, he almost didn't care. He wolfed it down and then finished off the water.

Roid and Aster stayed away for a long time. Clark finally realized they must have gone to school. He checked out the lock on the cage. If he had something sharp, it would be easy to open. After searching every inch of the cage, he gave up. There was no sharp object, but his eye was caught by something else.

Lying in the corner of the cage was a booklet titled *Taking Care of Your Ickie,* by the Bonezillion brothers. Clark opened it and began to read:

1. Ickies love to play ball. Buy a special ball for only ½ bone!
2. Feed and water your Ickie daily. Buy a box of food for only 2 bones!
3. Ickies love sugar. Sugar cubes are only ⅛ bone each!
4. Comb your Ickie every morning. Combs are just 1 bone each!
5. Ickies love friends. So why not buy another one today!

There was a note at the bottom in tiny letters. Clark squinted to read it: "Caution . . ." Just then, he heard the doorknob turn. He

dropped the booklet and pretended to be asleep.

"Quark," a voice said softly. "Are you awake?"

"Roid!" Clark cried, leaping back up. "Boy, am I glad to see you. Get me out of here."

Roid peeked both ways in the hall and then tiptoed inside Aster's room.

"Is school over?" asked Clark, once Roid had let him out of the cage.

"Third grade is. Sixth grade doesn't let out until three. So Aster Disaster won't be home for fifteen more minutes."

Roid tore up tissue and littered it around the room as he spoke. Then he frayed a ribbon lying near the cage.

"What are you doing?" Clark wanted to know.

"Making a mess, so Aster will think you did it." Roid stepped back and viewed his destruction with satisfaction. "When she sees this, she'll beg me to take you off her paws."

"Or she might clobber me instead," said Clark, looking on in horror.

"Uh-oh." Roid hesitated. "I hadn't thought of that."

"Great!" groaned Clark, slapping a hand to his forehead. "Well, think about it now, why don't you?"

Suddenly they heard someone clomping up the stairs.

"It's Aster! She's home early," whispered Roid.

Aster burst into her room. She looked at the tissue still in Roid's hand and then around at the mess he'd made.

"What are you doing?" she wailed. "Mom! Roid is destroying my room!"

"I didn't do it," Roid fibbed. "I was just

trying to clean up the mess your Ickie made."

"Aster! Roid!" called a voice from the hall.

The beagles' mother soon appeared in the doorway and frowned at the mess. "What happened in here?" she demanded.

"The Ickie did it," Aster told her quickly.

"I knew that pet would be nothing but trouble," their mom said with a sigh. "Maybe we should return it for a refund."

"Yes." Aster nodded. "I think so too. Then I could get a Snarkian Thumper instead."

No! thought Clark. The Interplanetary Shopping Network would probably just resell

him. He didn't want to take his chances with another owner. He gave Roid a "see what you did" look.

"Wait!" shouted Roid. "Give it to me. I'll train it to behave."

"I thought we'd decided you'd wait until fourth grade to get your own pet," said his mom.

"Pleeeease," begged Roid. "I'll take good care of it. I already walked it yesterday, and I fed it today."

"Well, okay," his mom agreed after a minute. "We'll give it a try since you want the Ickie so much."

"You're not getting it for free," Aster butted in.

"I'll swap you five bones for it," Roid offered.

"No deal. I paid six. Plus food, cage, and shipping. Eight bones, or I'm keeping it."

"Eight bones!" Roid protested. "That's a whole allowance!"

One allowance? thought Clark. Was that all he was worth?

"So? If you think it's too much, then go buy your own Ickie from the Shopping Network," said Aster.

"But the Bonezillion brothers won't get

another shipment for weeks," Roid argued.

Aster crossed her arms. "Eight bones. Take it or leave it."

Clark hoped Roid wasn't going to change his mind. He silently willed him to agree.

"Okay," Roid said finally. He reached for Clark, but Aster blocked him. She held out one of her paws. "Pay up first."

Roid dashed out of the room, leaving Aster and her mom behind with Clark.

"Oh, boy—can I get a Snarkian Thumper now?" Aster asked.

"I'm not sure you're ready for another pet. You didn't take very good care of this one," her mother replied.

"But everyone at school is getting a Thumper!" Aster whined. "And it's not my fault that the Ickie was so hard to take care of."

"I've heard that Thumpers are even more work than Ickies," her mother warned.

"Oh, come on. Please," Aster begged.

"I'll think it over," her mom said firmly as she turned and left the room.

All of a sudden, Clark was alone with Aster. He scurried back into the cage, pulling its door shut behind him.

Aster bent down to glare in at him. "This is all your fault," she grumbled.

"Hah!" muttered Clark.

Oops! He clapped his hands over his mouth. For a second, he'd forgotten he wasn't supposed to talk in front of her.

Aster looked surprised—then interested. Her face drew nearer until Clark could feel her warm, moist dog breath. Unfortunately, he could smell it too.

"Did you just say something?" she asked.

Clark kept quiet and tried to look stupid. He hoped Roid was hurrying with those bones.

Just then Roid dashed back in and dumped some bones in Aster's paw. Grabbing Clark's cage, he grinned at her. "It's been a pleasure doing business with you."

Clark gazed back at Aster as Roid carried him away. She looked as though she suspected she'd been tricked but wasn't quite sure how.

Clark couldn't help himself. He gave her a little wave. "So long, dogface," he called softly.

"Hey!" she yelled. "Roid! Wait—I changed my mind!"

Chapter 4

Safe!

Roid whisked Clark into his room, with Aster in hot pursuit.

"A deal's a deal," Roid told her. He tried to shut the door on her.

"But I didn't know it could talk," Aster objected.

"Talk? You must be imagining things." Roid shook his head. "I haven't heard it say anything. Gotta go . . ."

He managed to shut his door this time—with her on the outside.

"Phew! She had me worried for a minute

there," Roid said. He looked around his room thoughtfully. "Now, where do you want me to keep your cage?"

"Let's get something straight." Clark stuck his face up against the cage bars to glare at Roid. "First of all, I do not need a cage. Second of all, I'm not a pet."

"What do you mean?" asked Roid. "Of course you are."

"I'm not!" shouted Clark.

"Hold it down," Roid said soothingly. "You don't want my mom coming up here again, do you?" He set the cage on his desk and opened its door.

"I'm not a sea monkey!" Clark insisted, jumping out.

Roid flopped on his bed, head propped on one paw. "A what?"

"A sea monkey," Clark repeated, pacing to and fro on the desk. "On my planet, they sell sea monkeys in the back of comic books. They mail them to you all dried up. You just add water and they come back to life. At least I think that's how it works. My mom would never let me buy any. But my point is that I'm not just some sea monkey you can buy!"

"I didn't buy you first. Aster did," Roid pointed out. "I only rescued you from her."

"Did you ever stop to think about how worried my family must be?" Clark asked.

"No. Did you ever worry about the sea monkeys' families?" Roid answered.

"That's different," said Clark.

"How?" asked Roid.

Clark paused for a moment. Maybe it wasn't different. Maybe the sea monkeys had parents who worried about them when they disappeared. He didn't want to think about it.

"Take my word for it—it just is," Clark told him, sitting down on a stack of books. Roid didn't look convinced.

"You know, I was just about to get a baseball trophy when I was kidnapped," Clark went on. "There were nine other kids on my team. I think the Bonezillions kidnapped all of us. And then they sold us like we were animals!"

"You *are* an animal," said Roid.

"I'm not!" Clark protested. But then he remembered. "Oh, yeah, I guess I am. But how would you feel if you were kidnapped, freeze-dried, and transported to another planet to be somebody's pet?"

"Weird, I guess," Roid agreed. "But that would be different."

"Different how?" Clark asked.

"I don't know. It just would be," said Roid.

They stared at each other for a few seconds.

"Will you help me get back home?" Clark said finally.

"Home! To Ick? But I just paid eight bones for you!" Roid complained. "And besides, I wanted to enter you in the city pet show next week."

"What's first prize in the show?"

"A trophy, twenty-five bones, and a year's supply of pet chow."

Clark thought a second and then leaped up. "I have an idea. If I help you win the pet show, then will you help me get back home?"

"But—are you sure you couldn't learn to like it here?" asked Roid.

Clark nodded. "I'm sure."

Roid sighed. "Okay, but I don't know how we're going to get you all the way back to Ick."

"Let's ask the Bonezillion brothers," Clark suggested. "If they brought me here, they can send me back, right?"

"Mmmm." Roid hesitated. "Maybe."

"What do you mean—'maybe'?"

"Coming and going are two different things," said Roid. "But let's not borrow trouble." He got out the leash. "Let's go."

Chapter 5

Going to the Dogs

On his leash, Clark followed Roid to a building with a huge bone-shaped sign out in front:

THE BONEZILLION BROTHERS
INTERPLANETARY SHOPPING NETWORK
HEADQUARTERS

They entered the building. It was terribly noisy and busy inside, with salesdogs rushing about carrying packages and order slips.

All around them were TV screens. They were in the floor, the ceiling, the chair backs—everywhere! And smiling salesdogs were selling products on every one of them. Clark watched, sipping from the plastic water bottle Roid had bought for him.

". . . Got a doggone embarrassing flea problem? Try Flea-B-Gone and your troubles will be over! . . ."

". . . Learn speed barking in your spare time with BARKS-A-LOT. . . ."

". . . Use the fantastic DOG-TROTTER for just three days and watch those dog pounds begin to melt away. . . ."

". . . Get your POLICE DOG security system today! Available for home or office . . ."

". . . Cat got your tongue at parties? Try . . ."

It was all kind of hypnotizing.

Roid tugged Clark over to the salesdog they had seen in the Instant Ickie commercial.

"Who is top dog around here?" Roid asked.

"That would be me!" yelled the salesdog. "I'm Slick Bonezillion. My brother, Buck, and I own the Network. Can I help you?"

"I want to send this Ickie home," Roid told him. "But not until after the city pet show."

Slick Bonezillion flashed his blinding white smile. "Is there something wrong with it?" he bellowed.

Clark thought they yelled just on TV, but it

seemed salesdogs talked that way all the time.

"I don't think it likes it here. I think it wants to go home," said Roid.

"Sorry! We don't ship to Ick!" Slick boomed, his smile widening even more.

"But you have to go there to get more Ickies, don't you?" Roid asked.

"Amazingly—no!" the salesdog shouted. "We have discovered a patented laser-ray system for zapping pets here from other planets. So we never even have to visit the planets ourselves. This miraculous process is known as RayNap. And here's how it works. . . ."

He waved his hands like a magician doing

a magic trick. "First we send a probe to the other planets to locate pets. Then a RayNap ray transports the pets here to K-9 efficiently, safely, and effectively!

"As you may have heard, our first shipment of Ickies was an overwhelming success. Soon we hope to sell hundreds of Ickies a day all over the galaxy. Planets like Urp and Scud are always looking for pets."

"Eeew!" Roid made a face at Clark. "You're lucky you weren't sent to either of those planets."

"What's wrong with them?" Clark asked.

"Nothing if you don't mind heaps of garbage and the smell of burning rubber."

"Did that Ickie just talk?" asked Slick, leaning down to peer more closely at Clark.

"No!" Roid said quickly.

"Yes, it did!" insisted the salesdog. "Wow! Wait until I tell Buck about this. Our research didn't indicate that Ickies had such highly developed communication skills. Imagine— talking pets! Shoppers will pay a fortune for Ickies when word gets around."

"Let's get out of here," Clark muttered, starting to feel nervous.

"Stop them!" shouted Slick. "I want a video of the Ickie speaking."

Suddenly salesdogs came running from everywhere.

Roid and Clark dodged them and took off through a side exit. They just barely escaped.

On the way back to Roid's house, Clark started to worry about a new problem. Because of him, now the Bonezillion brothers might kidnap even more kids from Earth. They'd probably turn Earth into one giant intergalactic pet store.

He had to stop them! But how?

He glanced over at Roid. The big beagle was giving Clark a weird look.

"What's wrong?" asked Clark.

"You're getting taller," Roid said. "You were only up to my knees yesterday. But now you're up to my waist."

"It must be a growth spurt," Clark decided. "That sometimes happens to us Earth kids— I mean, Ickies."

Chapter 6

Fetch. Roll Over.
Good Boy, Clark!

"Can I go to school with you?" Clark asked Roid the next morning. "It's boring staying here all day by myself."

"We can only bring pets to school on Sharing Day," Roid explained.

"But what am I supposed to do while you're gone?"

"I don't know. Do whatever pets do while their owners are away."

"I used to have some fish. I wonder if they were bored in their bowl all day when I was at school?" Clark mused.

"Hmm, I never thought about pets having

pets. Interesting concept," said Roid. "Uh-oh. I'm gonna be late." And with that, he dashed out the door.

Clark had never thought about pets having pets either. But after Roid left, he had lots of time to think. He wondered if his dog had pets he didn't know about. Maybe Critter had a regular flea circus on his back that he trained every time Clark wasn't looking. Or maybe . . .

It seemed like forever, but Clark finally heard Roid return from school. He jumped up, glad he was about to have company again.

"Are you ready to practice your tricks for the pet show?" Roid asked after dumping his backpack on the desk.

"What kinds of tricks?" Clark replied doubtfully.

"Nothing too hard. I'm sure you can handle it. But let's go to the park to practice so Aster can't spy on us," Roid said.

It took them a while to reach the park. Dogs on the street kept stopping Roid to ask questions about his pet, and puppies kept stopping Clark so they could pet him.

"Ooooh! It's so cute!" cooed a little cocker spaniel puppy. "What's its name?"

"Quark," said Roid.

The cocker spaniel rubbed Clark's head. "Good boy, Quark."

"This is getting embarrassing," Clark whispered to Roid. "Let's get out of here."

They finally reached a grassy area with an arched entrance sign:

HYDRANT MEMORIAL PARK

"Ready to begin training?" Roid asked.

Clark looked around the park. There were trees, dirt, grass, and hydrants as far as the eye could see. And in the distance, waves crashed on a sandy beach. A dog paradise.

"I guess so," he said glumly.

"Okay, let's try an easy one first," Roid suggested.

He threw a rubber ball across the park. "Fetch!" he called.

Clark folded his arms and didn't move.

"Come on," Roid urged. "Don't you even know how to fetch? What kind of pet are you anyway?"

"I'm not . . ." Clark began.

Roid held up a paw. "Sorry, I forgot. You don't consider yourself a pet. I'll try to remember."

"Okay." Clark sighed. "Then I'll try to do your dumb pet tricks. But this is really going to be embarrassing."

"Great," said Roid. "Roll over, boy!"

Clark groaned.

As it turned out, though, Clark enjoyed the exercise. After they had finished, he drank thirstily from his water bottle. Then Roid tried to put Clark's collar and leash back on him before they went home.

"Hey, your collar's too small," said Roid. "Or actually—I think the problem is that you've gotten too big. You're almost as tall as I am!"

It was true, Clark realized. He was much taller than he had been just two days earlier. "This is not just a growth spurt. What's happening to me?"

They hurried home to search for clues in the booklet the Bonezillion brothers had sent with Clark.

"So that's it!" Roid said after studying the booklet.

Clark grabbed it from him. At the bottom of the last page, in tiny letters, he read: "Caution: Your Ickie may continue to adjust in size as it receives more water."

"The RayNap ray must have temporarily shrunk you," Roid guessed.

"And now all the water I've been drinking is making me grow again," Clark decided.

Roid looked at him doubtfully. "Exactly how big are you going to get? Hey, what if being on K-9 turns you into some kind of giant!"

Clark gulped. Yeah, what if?

Chapter 7

A Dog's Best friend

By the day of the pet show, Clark was twice as tall as Roid. He was even taller than Roid's mom. She wanted to call the Bonezillion brothers to complain, but Roid got her to agree to wait until after the pet show.

Roid made a new collar for Clark out of a bandanna and hooked his leash to that. Then they headed for the city fairgrounds.

After Roid registered them for the show, they waited impatiently while other pets performed tricks.

There was a Plutonian Wiggler that jumped through hoops.

Then a Wickie-Up from Planet Scud juggled six tires.

"You're much better than they are," Roid whispered to Clark.

"Gee, thanks," Clark replied, rolling his eyes.

When it was finally their turn, Clark followed Roid to the center of the show ring. Roid threw a rubber toy as far as he could and called out, "Fetch!"

Clark cartwheeled over to the toy, picked it up in his mouth, and then did handsprings back to Roid. He dropped the toy in Roid's paw and bowed to the crowd.

Everyone laughed and barked loudly with enjoyment.

Next Roid gave Clark a stick and then tossed a ball toward him. As if he were taking batting practice, Clark swung the stick and hit the ball as hard as he could. It sailed over the stands and out of sight.

The onlookers howled with excitement and barked even louder.

"For our last trick, my Ickie will speak," announced Roid. He turned to Clark. "Speak," he told him.

Clark spoke. "The Bonezillion brothers kidnapped me from my home! Do not buy pets from the Bonezillion brothers!"

The crowd went wild. When the mayor announced that Roid and Clark had won, the audience's barking and howling grew so loud that Clark had to cover his ears.

Watching Roid accept the trophy reminded Clark of his own last few moments on Earth. He missed his home. His family. His stuff.

The Bonezillion brothers dashed over to Clark and Roid after they'd received the trophy.

"Are you going to send me back home now?" Clark asked them. Surely they would be glad to get rid of him just to shut him up about their kidnapping scheme.

"Are you kidding!" yelled Slick Bonezillion. "Now that word is out that Ickies can talk, we'll sell millions!"

Slick was right, Clark realized. All the audience had seemed to care about was the fact that he could speak. They hadn't listened to what he'd actually said.

A poodle woman came over and smiled at Clark.

"Just watch this," Slick murmured to Clark and Roid. He turned to the poodle. "Madame, how would you like to have your own Ickie for the amazing low price of just forty bones?"

"Forty!" cried Roid. "What a rip-off."

"I wish I could buy one," said the poodle lady. "But that huge thing would eat me out of house and home in a week." She smiled an apology at Clark and trotted away.

For a very brief instant, the Bonezillion brothers stopped smiling. But then a German shepherd came by.

"How about you, sir?" Buck asked, beaming again. "Would you like to be the proud owner of an Ickie for just forty bones?"

"No way. It's cool, but it's too big. I live in a small apartment," said the shepherd. It turned away.

The Bonezillion brothers stopped smiling altogether. "It looks like no one wants to buy our Ickies when they get this big," Slick grumbled.

"If we can't unload them, we'll have to feed them ourselves. Buying all that Ickie chow will break us," Buck worried.

Just then a salesdog hurried over to Slick.

"Mr. Bonezillion, sir," he panted. "We've gotten complaint calls from Ickie owners all over the galaxy today. The Ickies are getting too big and eating too much. Nine of them have been returned." He pointed behind him.

All the other players from Clark's baseball team stood there. Clark ran up to them. They hugged one another and began discussing their adventures as fast as they could. Clark had never been so glad to see his friends in his life.

"What should we do with them?" the salesdog asked the Bonezillion brothers.

Clark whirled toward them. "Send us back home?" he suggested hopefully.

The Bonezillion brothers looked at each other and shrugged. Slick Bonezillion sighed. Buck Bonezillion huffed.

"I'll guess we'll have to take the loss," said Slick.

"No problem," Buck assured his brother. "I just got a tip that there are some great pets available on planet Twerp. We'll beef up our inventory again in no time."

He turned to Clark and the rest of his team. "Are you all ready?" he asked.

"You mean you're going to send us back home right now?" exclaimed Clark.

"No time like the present," said Slick.

"Is that ray going to shrink us again?" Clark asked cautiously.

"We have corrected that tiny flaw in the RayNap process," Buck told him. "Your size will remain constant. Now let's move it."

"Do you really have to go home?" Roid sounded wistful.

"Yes," said Clark. "It's where I belong. Besides, now that you have twenty-five bones, you can buy any pet you want."

Roid scratched his ear and sighed. "Yeah. But you're the best pet—oops, I almost forgot—I mean the coolest friend a dog could ever have."

Before Clark could reply, the Bonezillion brothers turned the RayNap beam on him and the rest of the team. Clark felt a tingle run through his body.

Suddenly Aster ran up. "That's *my* Ickie!" she shouted. "I want it back. The trophy should be mine."

"'Bye, Quark! I'll miss you!" Roid called, waving.

And as Clark raised his hand to wave back, Roid and Aster faded right before his eyes. . . .

The next thing he knew, Clark was back on Earth.

He looked around. He was standing onstage with the baseball trophy in his hands. The rest of his team was there too. He and the others were the same size they'd always been on Earth.

The coach was smiling. The audience was still there. Almost nothing had changed. It was as though just a few seconds had passed since he'd left. Time on planet K-9 must move a lot faster than Earth time, Clark decided.

Right after the ceremony, Clark dashed home. He and the team had a lot to talk about after all they'd been through, but that could wait until tomorrow.

He ran through the white gate across the sidewalk in front of his house. His dog, Critter, came bounding up to him, barking like crazy and wagging his tail. Clark dropped to the ground, hugging Critter as they rolled around in the soft grass.

"I missed you . . . friend," he told the dog.

Critter licked Clark's face joyously in return.

It was good to be home.